Coast-to-Coast With Wally The Green Monster™

W9-BFR-612

Jerry Remy

Illustrated by Justin Hilton

MASCOT BOOKS®

www.mascotbooks.com

Wally The Green Monster wears number "97" on his Red Sox jersey to mark the year he was introduced as the team's mascot.

Wally The Green Monster was enjoying another season as the mascot of the Boston Red Sox. With the team on a long road trip, the lovable mascot decided it was a perfect time for a vacation. He wanted to visit Red Sox fans all over America and learn more about our great country. Wally packed his bags, took the wheel of the Wally mobile, and hit the road!

Wally drove south, stopping first in New York City. Although New York was home to Wally's rival baseball team, Wally enjoyed his time in the "Big Apple." He especially loved visiting the Statue of Liberty.

Wally continued south to Washington, D.C. — the capital of the United States of America. Wally stopped at the Washington Monument and the White House. Everywhere Wally ventured, he was instantly recognized by Red Sox fans cheering, "Hello, Wally!"

From the nation's capital, Wally continued south all the way to Florida. Wally dressed in his bathing suit and hit the beach. Wally made sure to use plenty of sunscreen so his green fur would not burn. The mascot relaxed on the sandy beach.

NASA space vehicles are launched from The John F. Kennedy Space Center located near Cape Canaveral, Florida.

Wally explored a swamp aboard an airboat. As he navigated through the marsh, he ran into several hungry alligators. "Yikes!" thought Wally. An alligator nearby chomped, "Hello, Wally!"

Ready for a real adventure, Wally The Green Monster went to The Kennedy Space Center, where he joined a crew of astronauts aboard the Space Shuttle. "Blast-off, Wally!" called an astronaut as they lifted high into the air.

Wally's next stop was Texas! Knowing that the rodeo was popular among Texans, Wally wanted to ride a bull … a mechanical bull! As he held on tight to stay on the bull, Wally's fans cheered, "Ride 'em, Wally!"

The world's largest rodeo and livestock event is held annually in Houston, Texas.

Texas, known as the "Lone Star State," is the second largest state in the country.

In San Antonio, Texas, Wally visited the The Alamo, where he learned about Texas history. He was happy to see Red Sox fans deep in the heart of Texas. The fans were surprised to see their favorite mascot so far from home. They cheered, "Howdy, Wally!"

Located in Northern Arizona, the Grand Canyon National Park was one of the first national parks in the United States.

Wally the Green Monster continued his coast-to-coast journey with a stop at the world-famous Grand Canyon in Arizona. The breathtaking canyon views amazed Wally. Not surprisingly, Wally ran into a family of Red Sox fans. The family called, "Hello, Wally!"

At the Grand Canyon, Wally enjoyed the great outdoors. He hiked on dusty trails and went rafting on the Colorado River. However, his favorite activity was riding a pack mule to the bottom of the canyon. Wally's mule was thrilled to be carrying such a famous mascot. The mule asked in a tired voice, "Are we there yet, Wally?"

Los Angeles, the second largest American city, means "City of Angels" in Spanish.

Wally's cross-country adventure took him next to California and the shores of the Pacific Ocean. The mascot first traveled to Los Angeles, where he began searching for movie stars. Wally received a hero's welcome in Hollywood, and was honored with his very own star on the famous Hollywood Walk of Fame. Wally fans cheered, "Bravo, Wally!"

When the Golden Gate Bridge was completed in 1937,
it was the longest suspension bridge in the world.

From Southern California, Wally made his way north to
the Bay Area. At the Golden Gate Bridge, Wally ran
into two young Red Sox fans. The young fans cheered,
"Hello, Wally!"

From California, Wally continued his adventure aboard a cruise ship headed for the Hawaiian Islands. When Wally arrived on the island of Oahu, he hopped on a surfboard and caught some waves. Hawaiians were impressed by his surfing abilities. They cheered, "Surf's up, Wally!"

Hawaii became the fiftieth (and last) state to join the United States in 1959.

From the tropical paradise of Hawaii, the cruise ship continued toward the cold waters of the North Pacific Ocean. Off the coast of Alaska, he watched huge whales splash out of the ocean. The whales called, "Hello, Wally!"

Back on land, Wally continued north toward the Arctic Circle by way of the Iditarod Trail. Several hard-working dogs pulled Wally and his sled over the snow-covered Alaskan landscape. The dogs barked, "Hello, Wally!"

The most famous dog sled race in the world is the Iditarod Trail Sled Dog Race, which is held annually in Alaska.

Seattle's Space Needle, built for the 1962 World's Fair, stands over 600 feet tall and is the most famous landmark in the Pacific Northwest.

After a few cold days in Alaska, Wally traveled south to Washington State. In Seattle, Wally visited the Space Needle and enjoyed spectacular views of the Puget Sound, Downtown Seattle, and snow-capped mountain ranges. Wally also relaxed at a local coffee shop, where he sipped a latte and read all about the Red Sox road trip.

Aware that Seattle was known for its rock-and-roll scene, Wally grabbed a guitar and joined a band on a nearby stage. Wally's fans cheered, "Rock on, Wally!"

From Seattle, Wally traveled to the lush forests of the Pacific Northwest. Lumberjacks taught Wally the sport of log rolling. Wally sure was a fast learner! As one lumberjack lost his balance and splashed into the water, he said, "You got me, Wally!"

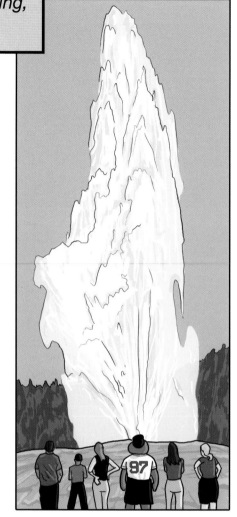

From the Pacific Northwest, Wally ventured east to Yellowstone National Park. At Old Faithful, Wally was amazed at how the geyser erupted like clockwork – every ninety minutes. Being in the wilderness, Wally was excited to set up camp and spend a night under the bright stars. Unfortunately, he received an unexpected visit from a grizzly bear! "Yikes!" thought Wally, as he ran for safety. The bear roared, "Hello, Wally!"

Wally continued east to South Dakota and Mount Rushmore National Memorial. Wally was impressed with the sculptures honoring presidents Washington, Jefferson, Roosevelt, and Lincoln. Wally wondered when the President of Red Sox Nation, his dear friend Jerry Remy, would be added to the mountainside!

Mount Rushmore National Memorial in South Dakota honors United States Presidents George Washington, Thomas Jefferson, Theodore Roosevelt, and Abraham Lincoln.

Construction on the Sears Tower was completed in 1973. Standing at 1,451 feet from the ground, it is the tallest skyscraper in the United States.

The next stop for Wally The Green Monster was Chicago, Illinois. Wally wanted to get a good look at Chicago, so he headed to the observation platform atop the Sears Tower. Wally was amazed at how far he could see in every direction from the tallest building in America.

Wally explored Chicago on the local train system called the "L." Wally hadn't yet found time to buy Red Sox players souvenirs, so he strolled along the "Magnificent Mile" on Michigan Avenue and bought gifts for his teammates.

Finally, Wally took a sailboat on Lake Michigan. It sure was windy on the lake! Seagulls flying overhead squawked, "Hello, Wally!"

Chicago is on the banks of Lake Michigan and is nicknamed the "Windy City."

Ice Hockey is the national winter sport of Canada.

Wally continued his tour of the Great Lakes region by crossing the border into Canada. Wally laced up his skates and joined a game of ice hockey. Wally impressed the locals with his skating and his ability to handle the puck. Wally scored a goal for his team! Surprised by Wally's hockey skills, his teammates asked, "You've played hockey before, eh?"

In curling, teams attempt to guide a 44-pound stone to a target on the far end of a 146-foot ice surface.

Niagara Falls is situated along the border between Canada and the United States and attracts over 20 million visitors annually.

While Wally was comfortable on skates, he had never tried his hand at the sport of curling. The mascot gently guided the curling stone down the ice. With the help of his teammates, who brushed the ice in front of the moving stone, Wally hit his target!

Wally's next stop was Niagara Falls. Wally learned that the falls are situated right on the Canadian-American border, with one fall in Canada and the second in America. Wally was surprised at how close he was able to get to the water. Wally noticed Red Sox fans through the misty air. The fans cheered, "Hello, Wally!"

After a fun-filled vacation, Wally finally made his way back to Boston, Massachusetts, and his home in Fenway Park. The mascot ran into many Red Sox fans on Yawkey Way who had started to gather for the baseball game. Seeing so many great places and visiting so many Boston Red Sox fans along the way, Wally The Green Monster felt like the luckiest mascot in the world.

Coast-to-Coast With
Wally The Green Monster

To my favorite Wally fan, my grandson, Dominik. ~ Jerry Remy

For my Parents ~ Justin Hilton

For more information about our products,
please visit us online at www.mascotbooks.com.

Copyright © 2008, Mascot Books, Inc. All rights reserved.
No part of this book may be reproduced by any means.

Mascot Books, Inc.
P.O. Box 220157
Chantilly, VA 20153-0157

Major League Baseball trademarks and copyrights are used
with permission of Major League Baseball Properties, Inc.

ISBN: 1-934878-08-1

Printed in the United States.

www.mascotbooks.com

MASCOT BOOKS
www.mascotbooks.com

Title List

Baseball

Boston Red Sox	Hello, *Wally*!	Jerry Remy
Boston Red Sox	*Wally The Green Monster* And His Journey Through *Red Sox Nation*!	Jerry Remy
Boston Red Sox	Coast to Coast with *Wally The Green Monster*	Jerry Remy
Boston Red Sox	A Season with *Wally The Green Monster*	Jerry Remy
Colorado Rockies	Hello, *Dinger*!	Aimee Aryal
Detroit Tigers	Hello, *Paws*!	Aimee Aryal
New York Yankees	Let's Go, *Yankees*!	Yogi Berra
New York Yankees	*Yankees* Town	Aimee Aryal
New York Mets	Hello, *Mr. Met*!	Rusty Staub
New York Mets	*Mr. Met* and his Journey Through the Big Apple	Aimee Aryal
St. Louis Cardinals	Hello, *Fredbird*!	Ozzie Smith
Philadelphia Phillies	Hello, *Phillie Phanatic*!	Aimee Aryal
Chicago Cubs	Let's Go, *Cubs*!	Aimee Aryal
Chicago White Sox	Let's Go, *White Sox*!	Aimee Aryal
Cleveland Indians	Hello, *Slider*!	Bob Feller
Seattle Mariners	Hello, *Mariner Moose*!	Aimee Aryal
Washington Nationals	Hello, *Screech*!	Aimee Aryal
Milwaukee Brewers	Hello, *Bernie Brewer*!	Aimee Aryal

College

Alabama	Hello, Big Al!	Aimee Aryal
Alabama	Roll Tide!	Ken Stabler
Alabama	Big Al's Journey Through the Yellowhammer State	Aimee Aryal
Arizona	Hello, Wilbur!	Lute Olson
Arkansas	Hello, Big Red!	Aimee Aryal
Arkansas	Big Red's Journey Through the Razorback State	Aimee Aryal
Auburn	Hello, Aubie!	Aimee Aryal
Auburn	War Eagle!	Pat Dye
Auburn	Aubie's Journey Through the Yellowhammer State	Aimee Aryal
Boston College	Hello, Baldwin!	Aimee Aryal
Brigham Young	Hello, Cosmo!	LaVell Edwards
Cal - Berkeley	Hello, Oski!	Aimee Aryal
Clemson	Hello, Tiger!	Aimee Aryal
Clemson	Tiger's Journey Through the Palmetto State	Aimee Aryal
Colorado	Hello, Ralphie!	Aimee Aryal
Connecticut	Hello, Jonathan!	Aimee Aryal
Duke	Hello, Blue Devil!	Aimee Aryal
Florida	Hello, Albert!	Aimee Aryal
Florida	Albert's Journey Through the Sunshine State	Aimee Aryal
Florida State	Let's Go, 'Noles!	Aimee Aryal
Georgia	Hello, Hairy Dawg!	Aimee Aryal
Georgia	How 'Bout Them Dawgs!	Vince Dooley
Georgia	Hairy Dawg's Journey Through the Peach State	Vince Dooley
Georgia Tech	Hello, Buzz!	Aimee Aryal
Gonzaga	Spike, The Gonzaga Bulldog	Mike Pringle
Illinois	Let's Go, Illini!	Aimee Aryal
Indiana	Let's Go, Hoosiers!	Aimee Aryal
Iowa	Hello, Herky!	Aimee Aryal
Iowa State	Hello, Cy!	Amy DeLashmutt
James Madison	Hello, Duke Dog!	Aimee Aryal
Kansas	Hello, Big Jay!	Aimee Aryal
Kansas State	Hello, Willie!	Dan Walter
Kentucky	Hello, Wildcat!	Aimee Aryal
LSU	Hello, Mike!	Aimee Aryal
LSU	Mike's Journey Through the Bayou State	Aimee Aryal
Maryland	Hello, Testudo!	Aimee Aryal
Michigan	Let's Go, Blue!	Aimee Aryal
Michigan State	Hello, Sparty!	Aimee Aryal
Minnesota	Hello, Goldy!	Aimee Aryal
Mississippi	Hello, Colonel Rebel!	Aimee Aryal

Pro Football

Carolina Panthers	Let's Go, Panthers!	Aimee Aryal
Chicago Bears	Let's Go, Bears!	Aimee Aryal
Dallas Cowboys	How 'Bout Them Cowboys!	Aimee Aryal
Green Bay Packers	Go, Pack, Go!	Aimee Aryal
Kansas City Chiefs	Let's Go, Chiefs!	Aimee Aryal
Minnesota Vikings	Let's Go, Vikings!	Aimee Aryal
New York Giants	Let's Go, Giants!	Aimee Aryal
New York Jets	J-E-T-S! Jets, Jets, Jets!	Aimee Aryal
New England Patriots	Let's Go, Patriots!	Aimee Aryal
Seattle Seahawks	Let's Go, Seahawks!	Aimee Aryal
Washington Redskins	Hail To The Redskins!	Aimee Aryal

Basketball

Dallas Mavericks	Let's Go, Mavs!	Mark Cuban
Boston Celtics	Let's Go, Celtics!	Aimee Aryal

Other

Kentucky Derby	White Diamond Runs For The Roses	Aimee Aryal
Marine Corps Marathon	Run, Miles, Run!	Aimee Aryal
Mississippi State	Hello, Bully!	Aimee Aryal
Missouri	Hello, Truman!	Todd Donoho
Nebraska	Hello, Herbie Husker!	Aimee Aryal
North Carolina	Hello, Rameses!	Aimee Aryal
North Carolina	Rameses' Journey Through the Tar Heel State	Aimee Aryal
North Carolina St.	Hello, Mr. Wuf!	Aimee Aryal
North Carolina St.	Mr. Wuf's Journey Through North Carolina	Aimee Aryal
Notre Dame	Let's Go, Irish!	Aimee Aryal
Ohio State	Hello, Brutus!	Aimee Aryal
Ohio State	Brutus' Journey	Aimee Aryal
Oklahoma	Let's Go, Sooners!	Aimee Aryal
Oklahoma State	Hello, Pistol Pete!	Aimee Aryal
Oregon	Go Ducks!	Aimee Aryal
Oregon State	Hello, Benny the Beaver!	Aimee Aryal
Penn State	Hello, Nittany Lion!	Aimee Aryal
Penn State	We Are Penn State!	Joe Paterno
Purdue	Hello, Purdue Pete!	Aimee Aryal
Rutgers	Hello, Scarlet Knight!	Aimee Aryal
South Carolina	Hello, Cocky!	Aimee Aryal
South Carolina	Cocky's Journey Through the Palmetto State	Aimee Aryal
So. California	Hello, Tommy Trojan!	Aimee Aryal
Syracuse	Hello, Otto!	Aimee Aryal
Tennessee	Hello, Smokey!	Aimee Aryal
Tennessee	Smokey's Journey Through the Volunteer State	Aimee Aryal
Texas	Hello, Hook 'Em!	Aimee Aryal
Texas	Hook 'Em's Journey Through the Lone Star State	Aimee Aryal
Texas A & M	Howdy, Reveille!	Aimee Aryal
Texas A & M	Reveille's Journey Through the Lone Star State	Aimee Aryal
Texas Tech	Hello, Masked Rider!	Aimee Aryal
UCLA	Hello, Joe Bruin!	Aimee Aryal
Virginia	Hello, CavMan!	Aimee Aryal
Virginia Tech	Hello, Hokie Bird!	Aimee Aryal
Virginia Tech	Yea, It's Hokie Game Day!	Frank Beamer
Virginia Tech	Hokie Bird's Journey Through Virginia	Aimee Aryal
Wake Forest	Hello, Demon Deacon!	Aimee Aryal
Washington	Hello, Harry the Husky!	Aimee Aryal
Washington State	Hello, Butch!	Aimee Aryal
West Virginia	Hello, Mountaineer!	Aimee Aryal
Wisconsin	Hello, Bucky!	Aimee Aryal
Wisconsin	Bucky's Journey Through the Badger State	Aimee Aryal

Order online at **mascotbooks.com** using promo code " **free**" to receive **FREE SHIPPING**!

More great titles coming soon!

info@mascotbooks.com